When Santa Claus receives Christmas letters from children he becomes very busy preparing for Christmas Eve. But **that** is the busiest night of all for Santa Claus, as this simple story describes. Can he deliver all the presents before young children everywhere wake up on Christmas morning?

Available in Series S846 Square format Bible Stories
The First Christmas

British Library Cataloguing in Publication Data
Bradbury, Lynne
   Santa Claus has a busy night.
   I. Title   II. Davis, Jon
   823'.914[J]   PZ7
   ISBN 0-7214-9531-1

First Edition

Santa Claus
has a busy night

written by LYNNE BRADBURY
illustrated by JON DAVIS

Ladybird Books Loughborough

Santa Claus had been busy for weeks.
He had had hundreds of letters from boys and
girls, all telling him what presents they would
like for Christmas.

He had sorted out the letters
and made a long, long list...

dolls
bikes
puzzles
books
clothes
boats
planes
paints
watches
radios
computers
trains
games
skates
pencils
balloons

And then, on the other side, he had
written the children's names and
where they lived so that he would
know where to go.

At last it was Christmas Eve, the night before Christmas. Santa Claus had been even busier that day, filling his sacks and loading them onto his sleigh.

He had fed his reindeer and now they were
standing together, ready to pull the heavy load.
Rudolph, with his bright red nose, was at the
front to lead the others.

Then Santa Claus went to get ready.

First he put on
his red trousers.

Then he put on
his red coat.

Next he put on
his red hat.

And last, he put on
his big black boots.

By now all the children would be going to bed.

Santa Claus hoped that they would soon be asleep.

He had so many places to visit.
It was time to go...

Up, up into the sky!
Through the clouds and back down over
sleeping towns and cities.

Down, down to the rooftops.
Santa Claus stopped his sleigh.

Then Santa Claus took one of his heavy sacks and climbed down the first chimney.

He filled the stockings (and even some pillow cases for big toys). Every time Santa Claus left a present, he ticked a name off on his list.

Some people left Santa Claus a mince pie or a piece of cake. He was very pleased. Climbing up and down chimneys made him feel hungry!

Being Santa Claus wasn't an easy job. There were houses where the chimneys were too small and houses with no chimneys at all.

Some children were sick and in hospital and others were staying at a different house. But Santa Claus didn't forget anyone.

He climbed hundreds of stairs and tiptoed in and out of dark rooms to leave his presents.

And all the time, Rudolph and the other reindeer pulled the sleigh from place to place.

Santa Claus went to places which
were cold and snowy – Brrr!

He went to places which were wet and windy – and he nearly lost his hat!

He flew over high mountains...

...over sandy deserts

...and over the sea.

On and on through the night sky flew
Santa Claus...

This time he was on his way to a hot country
where it was summer and not winter.

Phew! He wished that he could take off his thick red coat and his big furry boots. Christmas Day was going to be a very hot day for these children!

At last Santa Claus reached the last name on his list. He had finished. All the sacks were empty!

It would be daylight soon and the children would be waking up.
"Time to go home, Rudolph!" he said.

When Santa Claus got back home, the first thing he did was to feed his tired reindeer and put them to bed.

Then he went into his house, took off his hat, his coat and his boots and sat in his big chair by the fire.

It was Christmas Day.

Santa Claus thought about all the places he'd visited. By now all the children would be awake. He hoped that they would be pleased with their presents.

Some children hadn't been given *all* the things they'd asked for — Santa Claus couldn't carry any more.
Some children would remember to say thank you and others would forget. Oh well! And Santa Claus went to sleep... **but** there's one thing we've forgotten in this story —

who delivers presents to...

Santa Claus?